# DANCE AUDITIONS

By Tammy R. Nelson

First Printing: 2014

ISBN 978-1-4951-2787-8

Hoi Polloi Trends, LLC
5070 Village Green Drive
Mason, OH 45040

www.hoipolloitrends.com

Dedicated to my smart, talented, loving, funny and determined daughters…

Olivia, aka "Poptart"

and

Nora, aka "Pipes"

I love watching you both do what you love as you light up the stage with your incredible dancing for all of us to enjoy!

**Important note:**

**This book is not meant to be read cover to cover. Instead, this "game book" will ask you to make choices as you read the story. Each time you make a choice, you will be picking a new page to jump to— simply turn to the page indicated for the choice you've made.**

Remember—this book is just for fun! While some choices you make in this book will lead to positive outcomes and others will lead to less desirable ones, it is not intended as an educational piece on how to make good choices.

Finally, all characters appearing in this book are fictitious. Any resemblance to real persons, living or dead, is purely incidental.

~ ~ ~

**Let's get started! Your "Pick Your Page" story starts on page 6...**

Dance nationals are just a few weeks away but all the buzz at 5678 Shine Dance Studio is about next year's auditions. In classes this week, you've started to learn all the routines for tryouts. They look tricky this year!

You wonder how Paige seems to pick up the choreography so effortlessly. It seems like she must have already known all the moves with how fast she picks up the combinations. Since she's pretty much the best dancer at the studio, she probably doesn't have a lot to worry about at auditions.

You feel kind of bad for Stephanie, though. She seems shy and just moved here from Nebraska. She joined your classes just for this week so she could learn the routines for auditions. She has blonde hair and is very muscular. It seems like she must have had good training because her technique is strong, but she's having trouble remembering the combinations.

~ ~ ~

Continue on page 7.

The studio owner is changing all the teams for next year, so nerves are running high among you and your friends. Everyone wants to get placed on the top teams but, of course, everyone wants to stay with their friends, too. After all, besides school, 5678 Shine Dance is where you spend most of your life. It's your home away from home.

You're pretty sure that someday you want to be a professional dancer or to own a dance studio. You know that it's really hard to make it in the professional dance world or to start your own business, but you also know that anything is possible. Your mom always (somewhat annoyingly) reminds you of the quote by Audrey Hepburn, "Nothing is impossible. The word itself says 'I'm possible.'"

~ ~ ~

When you get home from dance classes, do you start practicing what you learned for auditions right away?

If yes, turn to page 11.

If no, turn to page 8.

Auditions are really important but they're still a couple weeks away and your last regional competition for *this* season is this weekend. You always want to do well at competition but your grandparents, brother, sister and one of your school friends will be there this weekend so there's extra pressure to do your best.

You're actually kind of surprised that you worked so much on the audition material in classes this week. Usually, the week before competition you work really hard to clean all the dances and make any last corrections in class.

You decide to spend your time getting ready for the weekend. You remember that there's a title competition at this one, too, so there will surely be some tough solo competition.

~ ~ ~

To see how the competition turns out, continue on page 9.

The competition went really well! You even nailed your triple turn and second turns in your solo (a big improvement over the last competition where it seemed you just couldn't find your center).

Out of 45 soloists in your age group you took first place and, for the first time ever, you won title! "Miss Junior Dance"—that really has a nice ring to it. You would have been happy with first place but the title and the crown—this was truly the proudest day of your life.

And, the best part—your whole family was there to cheer you on and share in your excitement!

~ ~ ~

After the glow subsides from the weekend, continue on page 10.

The next night at dance you hear the worst dance news you've ever heard. Your mom thought auditions were on Sunday afternoon but you just found out they are on Saturday in the middle of the day.

Your family is headed out of town right after school on Friday and not returning until midday Sunday. This trip has been planned for five months and your little cousins are looking forward to it as if it were Christmas morning.

When you talk to your teacher about the mix-up, she offers to do your audition right there on the spot, so you can go with your family out of town without having to worry about auditions.

~ ~ ~

If you're ready and want to do your audition right now, turn to page 14.

If you're not ready or don't want to do your audition right now, turn to page 13.

You know that the best way to remember choreography is to practice it right away so, when you get home, you search for the songs on your phone, ask your mom if you can download them and get right to work.

Well, if you want to call it "work" that is. Dance is pretty much your life so it's a lot more "fun" than it is "work." You pause because that reminds you of something you once heard about doing what you love, because then you'll never have to work a day in your life. With that in mind, you hope this dance thing works out!

Back to practicing…it's especially fun to work on new choreography right now because when you're at the end of the season, you have been doing the same dances over and over for competition.

~ ~˙~

If you stay up really late practicing, turn to page 12.

If you just practice an hour or so, turn to page 24.

The next morning, your dad isn't happy you stayed up so late dancing the night before because now you won't get out of bed for school.

And, he's about to be even more unhappy. When you finally roll out of bed, you realize you were so wrapped up in dance last night that you completely forgot to study for a science test and didn't get your math homework done.

Now you will have to stay after school, miss dance and, most important, you will miss learning the rest of the audition material! How can you audition without knowing the combinations?

~ ~ ~

Since you've danced at the same studio for several years, maybe they could place you on teams according to the teachers' knowledge of your skills. If you want to ask them if they'll do this instead of having you audition, turn to page 25.

If you'd rather "wing it" or try to figure out another option, turn to page 26.

Your heart is racing. How could you just audition on the fly? You haven't even practiced that much yet. You really want to be on the top team where most of your older friends and Paige will likely be placed. Dancing with her pushes you to be your best so you'd love to be on a team with her. Even though Paige is arguably the best dancer at the school, you can hold your own, and you even placed ahead of her at one of the competitions this year. The best way for the teachers to see this, is for you to audition together in the regular group auditions. Auditioning right now solo and unprepared may not be the best choice.

Your head is spinning when you get home. You really want to be with your family and visit your cousins but you don't want to miss auditions.

~ ~ ~

If you decide to beg your parents to stay home for auditions, go to page 16.

If you decide to go away with your family this weekend and do a private audition later, go to page 15.

Right now?! Your heart starts racing. You've been practicing all your audition combinations but you never expected to do them *today*.

But, you decide if you do it now and it goes well, it solves your problem. You get your audition completed and get to go out of town with your family this weekend.

You decide to go for it. You take a deep breath and tell yourself very confidently, "I can *do* this!"

And you do it. You really do it! The extra adrenaline from the stress pushes your leaps higher and makes your moves sharper. You remember all the choreography, your technique is strong and, most of all, your teacher is extra-impressed with how well you did under pressure.

As much as dance is your life, family is #1, and now you can go away for the weekend without any audition worries.

THE END

You hate to miss group auditions but, since your teacher offered to do a private audition when you return, you decide to go away with your family for the weekend.

Truth is, as much as your cousins are looking forward to seeing you, you might be looking forward to spending time with them even more. Your cousins are all younger than you, and you are crazy about babies!

You have so much fun hanging out with your family—lots of yummy food, a visit to a fun indoor play place and lots of laughs.

That evening you have the option to go swimming with your cousins or to go shopping with your mom and Grandma.

~ ~ ~

If you go swimming, go to page 17.

If you go shopping, go to page 18.

You know you should go with your family because that was planned long before auditions were scheduled, but you know it's better to audition with the group so your teacher can see how you dance with others and how you compare with others. Auditioning separately is risky and your family knows how much dance means to you so they'll probably understand.

So, you ask your mom about staying back for the weekend. She's disappointed about it but reluctantly agrees. You can tell she doesn't think it's the best choice but the worst part was actually your sister's reaction. She seems downright devastated. Your family is so busy that family weekends like this are rare and she was really looking forward to having *everyone* together.

~ ~ ~

If you change your mind and decide to go with the family for the weekend and do a private audition later, go to page 15.

If you decide you really need to stay back and go to auditions, go to page 19.

Swimming it is! You quickly change into your favorite swimsuit, grab your goggles and your flippers. Yes—flippers. Your older brother got you hooked on using them—hey, they make you go *really* fast.

You have so much fun with your cousins splashing and laughing and jumping. All the adults are down at the pool watching and having fun, too. There are lots of your favorite snacks to munch on and your brother helps you make all sorts of silly videos using a backwards camera app.

You are showing off your awesome toe touches when all the fun comes splashing to an end because you slip and sprain your ankle.

Now there won't be any auditions. Guess they'll just have to place you on teams based on what they know about your dancing from this year.

THE END

Even though you actually would have rather gone swimming, you haven't seen your grandma for awhile so you decide to go shopping with your mom and her. Plus, there might be another chance to swim later.

You go to an outside shopping area that has lots of great stores…for them. None of your favorite stores are there and you're starting to regret your decision when something amazing happens!

As you are headed out of a store, who was coming out of a store across the street but your favorite choreographer! You stop in your tracks stunned with excitement until your mom elbows you and says, "Come on! Let's go meet him!"

~ ~ ~

If you decide to ask for his autograph, go to page 32.

If you decide to ask for a picture with him, go to page 33.

You promise your sister that you will play school with her next weekend to make it up to her and stay behind for the weekend as your dad, brother and sister head out of town to see family.

Before you even have time to feel too bummed about it, you get a text from one of your friends saying she's going to have a get-together at her house that night.

You are immediately excited and want to go because you don't get to see your school friends that much. But, you have auditions tomorrow.

~ ~ ~

If you decide to go to the party, go to page 23.

If you decide to stay home, go to page 20.

You really want to go to the party but you also know you need to be responsible. The whole reason you're not with the rest of your family this weekend is because of auditions, so you decide you better stay focused on those.

Once your dad, brother and sister get to the hotel later that night, they FaceTime you and your mom so you can at least say "hi" to your cousins. As good as it was to see their sweet little faces, it makes you even sadder about not being there.

~ ~ ~

If you decide to just chill at home, go to page 21.

If you change your mind and decide to go to that party after all, turn to page 22.

Even though going to the party would help cheer you up, you know it's not the best move the night before auditions so you just relax on the couch. Minutes later you fall asleep. You don't wake up until almost midnight. You head upstairs to bed and sleep all the way through to morning.

Guess you really needed some sleep! You wake up refreshed and ready to go. You have time for a great breakfast and your mom offers to put your hair up in a cool style for auditions.

When you get to the studio you feel confident and ready to rock it! And boy did you! Your turns were clean, your leaps were strong and your performance was fierce. There's no doubt you'll be placed on the top teams, dancing alongside some of the studio's best.

THE END

What can it hurt? Since you can't be out of town with your family having fun with your cousins, you might as well go to the party. It's a lot better than moping around feeling sad.

It's not like you'd go to bed right now anyway. Your mom says it's OK so you decide to go to the party after all.

~ ~ ~

Continue to page 23.

When you get there, you find out lots of your best friends from school are there—even some from your classes last year. It's so great to see everyone. You painted each other's nails, did makeovers on each other and had a silly fashion show. Best part was there were lots of laughs. You're so glad you didn't miss this. It is just what you needed to cheer you up.

It's getting late and you know you should go home and get to bed but your friend's mom offers to let the party turn into a sleepover because everyone is having so much fun.

~ ~ ~

If you go home and get to bed before midnight, go to page 40.

If you decide to stay overnight and stay up until almost 3 a.m. having fun with your friends, turn to page 56.

You love dancing so much that you could literally dance all night long. But it's a school night. You really need to get your homework done and get some sleep, too.

With dance almost every day of the week, it's hard to balance it all but you wouldn't change it for anything. You just know you have to manage your time well—so you can get good grades and still do what you love most.

At least you were able to practice the audition combos for an hour. Now it's time for homework and then it's off to bed to rest up for a repeat tomorrow.

~ ~ ~

Continue to page 10.

Your dance teacher doesn't seem pleased, but agrees that they can place you without auditions, based on what they know of your dancing from this past year.

When the team lists come out, you're the one who's not too happy, though. You're on all the same teams as last year while most of your friends have moved up.

Without being at auditions, your teachers couldn't see you doing the new, more difficult choreography and didn't know how well you'd be able to keep up with the more senior dancers.

THE END

You're pretty resourceful so you figure you can think of another solution. Even though your teacher could probably place you based on what they know from this past year, you know you're up for a bigger challenge and want to show them that you can keep up with the more senior dancers like Paige.

The only way they'll be able to see this is if you learn the new, more complicated choreography and dance it side-by-side with the others.

You ask one of your best friends to record herself doing the routines from behind and send them to you so you can learn them, as if she's the teacher and you're behind her as the student learning them.

~ ~ ~

Continue to page 27.

The next day, at auditions, you're not feeling super confident since you learned the rest of the combinations from your friend instead of the teachers. What if she didn't have all the steps exactly right?

But, you're so happy she was willing to do that for you and she's a really good dancer so it must be at least 95% right. Considering you had only learned 50% of it, that was a big improvement.

As you thought about this and built up your confidence, you suddenly realize you forgot your tap shoes!

It's pretty hard to tap without tap shoes. And, because you do complicated moves on your toes, they need to fit exactly right, so borrowing shoes isn't an option.

~ ~ ~

If you decide to tell your teacher you forgot your shoes, go to page 28.

If you decide to call your mom about your forgotten shoes, go to page 29.

You decide that everyone makes mistakes and your teacher will probably understand so, while she's trying to get ready to start auditions, you tell her about the missing shoes.

Frustrated that you're interrupting her preparations with your problem, she reminds you that part of auditioning is coming to the audition ready to go.

She then pauses and it hits her that not only have you forgotten your tap shoes, but you weren't at the last practice to learn the rest of the audition routine.

She excuses you from the audition for being unprepared and says you'll just have to be happy with your placement based on what she knows from your work this past dance year.

THE END

When you're in a jam, Mom almost always has an idea that can help, so you give her a call. She's not very happy and points out that she can't make it all the way home to get your shoes and back to the studio before the auditions start.

Your mom realizes she is right near the dance store where you usually buy dance shoes, though. They would have your size and style on record. She offers to pick up new shoes and run them back to you if you're willing to pay her back. Expensive mistake, but you agree and Mom comes to the rescue.

Your confidence is really shaken now—you didn't even learn the combos from your teachers and now all this tap shoe stress! You don't want to look silly dancing "all out" if you're getting the steps wrong.

~ ~ ~

If you dance "all out" and perform with confidence, go to page 30.

If you play it safe but still dance really well, go to page 31.

You know it's always better to fully perform "all out," as they say, than to hold back because you are unsure of some of the choreography.

So you go for it. Just like the sign in your mom's office says, "All out. No regrets." You don't want to look back and think you could have danced it better.

You make a few mistakes throughout the auditions but your performance really stands out. Your teacher sees a side of your dancing that she hadn't seen before and thinks you're ready to dance up at the next level next year! You'll be on the top team with Paige and some of the other most experienced dancers at the studio.

THE END

Despite the setbacks with learning the material and forgetting your tap shoes, you danced really well. You didn't make many mistakes and your performance was solid. Not stand-out, but very solid.

After the audition, your teacher overheard one of your friends ask you how you learned the routines since you hadn't been in class. She heard you explain how you had asked another friend to record herself doing the combinations and how you had taught yourself from the videos.

Your teacher was really impressed with your determination and resourcefulness to find a way to learn the routines, even though you weren't able to come to class.

You ended up being placed on the teams you were hoping to be on and were even invited to dance up a level for one dance.

THE END

You muster up the courage and then blurt out, "May I please have your autograph?"

He signs the autograph but is actually kind of cold. He wasn't as friendly as you had expected. You blow it off thinking that it is probably somewhat annoying to get asked for an autograph all the time (although you secretly hope that that happens to you someday).

It was super exciting to meet him but not quite what you had dreamed of when you watched his choreography on "So You Think You Can Dance?" every week.

~ ~ ~

If you are still very gracious and thankful for the autograph and tell him about one of the dances he created that was your most favorite, go to page 34.

If you decide you've bothered him enough and just say a quick "thanks," go to page 35.

He agrees to take a selfie with you and then you tell him about one of the dances he created that was your most favorite.

You explain that you loved it because of all the incredible transitions, the partner work and all the unexpected movements that kept the audience on the edge of their seats.

~ ~ ~

Continue to page 34.

When you told him about the piece he choreographed that you loved, he instantly lit up! So many people just ask him for autographs and pictures because they saw him as a dancer on "So You Think You Can Dance?" and think he is "cute."

He takes his career very seriously and, while he loves to dance, choreography is his real passion. The fact that you were a fan of his choreography really opened up another side of him.

He invites you to his show that night and even gives you backstage passes to meet all the dancers and choreographers!

THE END

Well, that was cool. You don't get to meet a famous dancer and choreographer every day. Especially your favorite one!

After you part ways, you realize there *is* a store you're interested in at this mall after all. You head into the store that he had just come out of—a dance store called the Dance Nook.

You, your mom and your grandma really have fun in this store. They had fun finding cool dance outfits for you to try and you had a blast trying them all on. It was like a fashion show and you were the model! In the end, they bought you a really cool, unique dance outfit.

When you get back from shopping, there's still a little time before bed.

~ ~ ~

If you decide to use the time to get in a little practice for auditions, go to page 37.

Believe it or not, your cousins are still swimming. If you decide to join them and go swimming, go to page 17.

You were really thrown off when you slipped on that leap. And you *never* forget choreography. It's just not like you to fall and make mistakes.

This really put you in a foul mood and it showed in your dancing. You did the rest of the choreography correctly but played it safe because you didn't want to slip again, so your performance was flat.

Fortunately, you still make it onto the teams you were hoping for but you weren't invited to join any of the special small groups. Your teacher felt that you might not be able to handle all the stress of the extra dances since you crumbled after falling during auditions.

THE END

You figure your cousins must be almost done swimming by now anyway so you decide to get in a little practice for auditions. There's a dance floor at the hotel that they use for weddings but it's empty tonight so you are able to practice there.

After a short while, you are on a roll and get the choreography memorized well. You even spend some time stretching and get all the way down on your left splits for the first time!

As you fall asleep in the hotel room that night, you think about what you're going to wear to your private audition when you get back. You love the new outfit you got but it is really different—you haven't seen any of your friends wearing anything like it before.

~ ~ ~

If you decide to wear the new outfit, go to page 39.

If you decide to wear something you're a little more comfortable in (because you've worn it before and received compliments on it), go to page 38.

Who needs a flashy new outfit to do well in auditions? You decide to wear one of your favorite outfits that you're comfortable in that won't be distracting—after all, it's your dancing, not your outfit, that matters.

You are very focused and confident. You nail all the choreography and your kicks and leaps are extra high. The practice and stretching you did on the weekend really paid off.

You later find out that you made it on the team you had hoped for and are even invited to dance up a level for one dance with the seniors!

THE END

Even though you sometimes feel a little self-conscious in something unique, why get a new dance outfit and not wear it for a big day like your audition?

As you head out the door, your older teenage brother says, "Good luck" and then looks up from the piano. When he sees you he says, "Wow—cool outfit!" That was unexpected, and it gave you a great little boost of confidence. You snap a selfie and post it to Instagram with the caption, "A little nervous but #Ready4This in my new outfit from @DanceNook!"

At the audition you are really "on." It feels like you've known the choreography a lot longer than you have. It seems to flow effortlessly and you give your performance your all. The extra practice on the weekend really paid off!

On the way home you have a message from the Dance Nook, where you got the new dance outfit. They had seen your post on Instagram and asked if you'd be interested in modeling for their upcoming TV ads!

THE END

Your friends give you a little grief for being a "party pooper" but you don't care. You already had a great time at the party and you want to perform well at auditions tomorrow, so your mom comes to get you and you head home to bed.

~ ~ ~

Continue to page 41.

The next morning you get to auditions about 15 minutes early so you have time to stretch.

The new girl, Stephanie, looks stressed out. She seems to be having trouble remembering some of the choreography.

You know the choreography well but you got here early to stretch, not to run through the combinations.

~ ~ ~

If you get up from your stretching and help her run through the choreography, go to page 42.

If you're helpful and answer her questions but stay on the floor and keep focusing on your stretching, go to page 43.

If you were in Stephanie's shoes, you know you would really appreciate the help. So, you pop up from the floor with a smile and ask her if she wants to run through the combinations together.

Running through the choreography helped you warm up a little and it definitely helped her feel a little more comfortable.

You spent so much time helping her, though, that you ended up not having time to stop at the front desk and pick up your brand new jazz shoes. You were hoping to use them for the auditions but you'll have to just go with the old ones you're wearing.

~ ~ ~

Continue to page 45.

You really want to have strong kicks, leaps and jumps for the audition so you need to keep stretching, but you're happy to answer her questions while you're doing that.

You ask Stephanie if she's having trouble remembering any of the choreography. Shyly, she says, "Yes, what comes after the split leap?" You tell her the next few steps and answer a few more questions for her while you stretch.

Suddenly you remember that your mom had ordered your new jazz shoes and they were ready to be picked up at the front desk.

You stop stretching to go get them and then try to decide whether to wear them for the audition or not. They might help you do more turns. On the other hand, they could be slippery for leaps and jumps.

~ ~ ~

If you decide to wear your new shoes, go to page 44.

If you decide to stick with your old shoes for the audition, go to page 45.

Just as you had hoped, those new shoes made four turns feel as easy as a triple! You really rocked all your turns during the auditions—not only were you able to do more than usual, but you seemed to have even more control—probably because you weren't pushing so hard to make all the turns.

But, as you feared, they were slippery and you fell on one of your leaps. And then, to make matters worse, the surprise of the fall made you completely forget part of the choreography.

~ ~ ~

If you're able to brush it off and not let it bother you, go to page 46.

If the mistakes make you lose your confidence, go to page 36.

As it turns out, your old shoes with the hole in them should be renamed your "lucky" shoes because you have a great audition!

You stood out as a leader during the audition because you had lots of confidence and knew the choreography well. If anyone had a little trouble, they looked to you to remind themselves of the steps. And, because you were poised and knew the material, you were able to perform the combinations with a lot of character.

~ ~ ~

If you're so excited afterward that you decide to post a quick video from the audition on Facebook, go to page 48.

If you decide to call your dad, instead, to see if you can go out for pizza with some of your friends, go to page 47.

Mistakes happen. You know you have to brush it off so it doesn't affect your whole audition.

Just as you're pumping yourself back up, you see Paige forget some of the choreography. You honestly can't even believe it—everyone knows she's the best dancer at the school.

You know the part she forgot, but you're still off to the side trying to quickly remember the part you forgot before you have to run it again.

~ ~ ~

If you keep running through the part you forgot because you think she'll figure out her part, go to page 54.

If you stop working on your part and help her with the part she forgot, go to page 55.

Forget about Facebook, you want to hang out with your friends. You call your dad and he says you can go for pizza, so you catch a ride with one of your friends and her mom.

Everyone is so happy to have the auditions behind them that you all have an extra-fun time at the pizza place. Everyone is reminiscing about some of the funny things that happened during the season and talking about how much fun you'll all have at nationals.

Then the conversation turned to auditions and what combinations were the most difficult. That reminds you of the new girl, Stephanie.

~ ~ ~

If you bring her up in the conversation, go to page 49.

If you decide to just let the conversation go on without talking about her, go to page 50.

The next morning, you receive a message from a local ad agency. They saw your audition video on Facebook because you had tagged your dance studio in the post. They want to know if you and your dance friends would be interested in helping out with a flash mob on Fountain Square next weekend. The best part—you and your friends will even be paid for the job!

THE END

You mention that you thought Stephanie seemed nice and that she did a great job, especially considering she wasn't as used to the teachers' choreography styles as they all were.

Your friends agreed and one of them suggested that you should have invited her to join them at the pizza place. It was so crazy afterward and it was such a last-minute decision to go out for pizza, no one had thought of inviting her.

~ ~ ~

If you decide to send her a text and invite her to stop by, go to page 52.

If you decide that it's kind of late to ask her to join you since you've already ordered the pizza, go to page 53.

You decided to not bring up Stephanie because you weren't sure about what everyone thought of her. You didn't want anyone to say anything negative about her (You figure it's hard enough to be the "new girl" without having people talking about you.)

You realize you probably should have invited her to join you but she may have felt left out anyway since everyone was talking about the dance year and nationals.

~ ~ ~

Continue to page 51.

Before you leave the pizza place, one of your friends pulls up the 5678 Shine Dance website and sees that the results are already posted. You all crowd around her phone, shouting, "Read it! Read it! Tell us what teams we're on! Hurry up!"

Through all the excitement, she manages to read off all the teams and who is on each. You're really happy because you made it on all the teams you had hoped for and even found out that Stephanie will be dancing with you this year, too. It's too bad you didn't invite her for pizza so you could have gotten to know her better, but you feel happy that you helped her out before auditions and are looking forward to getting to know her better very soon!

THE END

Stephanie is thrilled to be included and, luckily, she lives really close to the pizza place! Her mom brings her right over to join the group—she even made it there before the pizza arrived.

Before leaving, Stephanie's mom thanks you for inviting Stephanie to join you and tells everyone that she is the new ballet teacher at the school. What a surprise! You knew there would be a new ballet teacher that year but had no idea it was her!

That explains why her technique was so good—she has a dance teacher for a mom! The group had a great time learning all about Stephanie, her old dance school and what her mom was like as a dance teacher.

Before you leave the pizza place, one of your friends pulls up the 5678 Shine Dance website and sees that the results are already posted. You are all excited to see that Stephanie will be on your team next year!

THE END

The next day you find out that someone from your studio invited Stephanie over to her house after auditions and now they're going to be doing a duet next season.

You're happy someone invited her over and she found a duet partner but are disappointed it wasn't you. You're still in search of a duet partner for next year and she would have been a perfect match for you—if only you had gotten to know her sooner!

THE END

Just as you had thought, Paige figured out the part she had forgotten and performed it beautifully when given a second chance. She's an amazing dancer and didn't need your help. It might have been a nice way to get to know her better, though.

That said, you were glad you spent the time to figure out your mistake because you, too, were able to remember the part you had forgotten the second time through. You even managed the leap without slipping in your new shoes this time.

The rest of the auditions went incredibly well and you are pleased to find out that you made it on the teams you were hoping for and even get to do one dance with Paige next year!

THE END

Paige was having a total brain-freeze and was so thankful for your help before she had to run that part again. And, by taking your mind off the part you were trying to remember for yourself, it instantly popped back in your head—you were just over-thinking it.

Both of you did a great job on the choreography you had missed the first time around.

After the auditions were done, your teacher asked you to stay behind. She said she had noticed how you managed to keep a positive attitude after your fall and forgetting the choreography. And she was really impressed that you reached out and helped Paige.

She asked if you would be interested in helping her as a student teacher next season because you demonstrated the kind of leadership and attitude she wanted her younger students to have.

THE END

A sleepover sounded like a great idea last night but when the alarm on your phone goes off in the morning you wish you hadn't stayed up so late. How will you ever have enough energy and focus to perform well at auditions?

You quickly shower, put on your dance clothes and put your hair up in a bun. When you arrive at the studio you stretch and try to get your energy up so you can perform well. It's too bad you don't like coffee.

During auditions you remember the combinations pretty well but you really don't feel like you did your best. You were falling out of your turns, your jumps weren't very high and, worst of all, your performance was just kind of flat.

All you can do now is hope that your teacher gives some weight to your performances this past year and doesn't base your placement for next year on just this audition.

THE END

# About the author

Tammy Nelson has been a marketer for more than 20 years, working at ad agencies and several Fortune 500 companies. She has an MBA from the Carlson School of Management. Her marketing research has been published in the *Journal of Consumer Marketing* but she has always wanted to write a book of her own. A promise made to her dancing

daughters (left) led to this dream come true. She and her family call Wisconsin home but are currently enjoying all Cincinnati has to offer. In addition to family activities with her husband and three kids, she enjoys photography, boating, dance, music and travel.

Made in the USA
Middletown, DE
01 December 2019

79762433R00033